PERPETUAL

A HARD SCI-FI FUTURE TECH NOVELETTE

M. LACEY

Story Builds

Story Builds Creative
2680 Baptist Road, Nesbit, MS 38651
Story-Builds.com

ISBN (digital): 978-0-9998725-7-4
ISBN (paperback): 978-0-9998725-8-1

Cover design, formatting, and production by Story Builds Creative.

CONTENTS

A global pandemic changes everything. What happens next? "Remnant, A Post-Pandemic Dystopian Tale" is the survival journal of two siblings after the fourth wave of this disease has swept the United States, and possibly the world.

Jump to the end of this book to get a sneak peak!

Michael consistently shares his newest short stories (and sometimes novels) with his subscriber list.

Join now! at fiction.MichaelLacey.me

Titles include:

"Perpetual: A Hard Sci-Fi Future Tech Novelette"
"Remnant,:A Post-Pandemic Dystopian Tale"
"Orphan Circus"
"Thirteen's Last Christmas: An Underland Adventure"
"Road Trip Reunion"
"Midnight Ride through Time"
"The Owl and the Acorn"

CHAPTER ONE_

I'm a perp. When I got older and actually cared about
history, I found out that wasn't a name people were
proud to have a few decades ago, but most people today
are perps. It's short for 'perpetual.' We wear collectors
that harness the power created by our movement. It's so
normal now it's hard to imagine a world without them.

The collectors are getting harder to move with each
upgrade, but that also means more power created. It's all
good except for the fact that we don't get paid any more
for the extra output.

Sure, some people have hacked older systems to still
work, but they usually don't get past the check stations,
and they have a hard time accessing any of their
currencies, either in power or coin. I avoid the older
models. I have a theory that the first generation collectors
might have something to do with the degenerative disease

called Ohm's that people have been getting lately. And I'm not the only one who thinks so.

There are a few people out there running around without collectors, but if you ask me, it's a waste. They can't get restaurant access or memberships without an approved wrist server, and you have to have collectors to make those work. Those people have no way to access their credits without an officially licensed unit.

The latest series of collectors is a slimline set called "Silk 2.0." I've never worn actual silk, but I imagine it's nothing like these new pieces. My collectors are secondhand from a few generations back; I've knee braces, ankle monitors, elbow guides, and wrist readers. Since I'm a bit of an overachiever, I upgraded to the neck rider and hip huggers, which produce decent power as they cover muscle groups from quads in my upper legs to my abs and lower back. I do regret not getting the gloves. Then, there's the capacitor. Because of all the collector upgrades, I had to go cheap on my cap. Capacitors are basically like batteries that store power temporarily until I transfer it to a bank.

With all these collectors, I ran out of credits for slim-caps, so I had to choose an older cap-pack, which is just a big capacitor that looks like a giant fire extinguisher on my back. It holds a lot, but it's the most god-awful contraption.

It's hard work to keep moving all day, but from what I've heard, it's a better living than most people had only a few generations ago.

On my way to the biggest bank—the one by the rail station pays the best locally—I notice someone staring at me. I'm hardly worth noticing except for my giant cap-pack. These are the times I wish I had the slim-caps, lining my arms and legs. This tank is a giant target for a siphoner.

Of course, if I had caps all around me, I'd look like a muscled up beast—not that I'm small by any means. It would still be safer than what I have. However, the cost of slim-caps to store as much juice as I can in my nearly classic cap-pack would've set us back to the beginning, like it was when my sister found out she also had Ohm's disease too. I wondered if it could be hereditary, but there's no evidence to support that yet.

When I need quick credits, I walk through a public collection park. There's a decent walking park a block away, but it pays a fraction of what the rail station does. Sure, it's faster, more convenient, and possibly safer, but I really need to get top dollar. With only one perp left in our house now, I can't afford to get less than the best for this energy.

As I round the next corner, I use a busted window's reflection to watch my back. The guy is definitely following me. No one takes this route, not even locals. It adds about a minute to the walk but is usually more peaceful since it's more isolated. I realize my mistake right away. In trying to see if he was after my power, I walked right into a situation that could hand it over.

Rather than waiting to know for sure, I quicken my gait to a light jog. This is common for perps since it fills the tanks faster, topping them off just before a paydock. The downside is that it could give away the fact that I'm nearly full up on power. I glance down to read 98% on my meter.

Maybe I should slow down. If I hit full capacity, then any extra work is wasted.

Once, I pushed my cap at 100% for a full day to see if it could hold more or if there was an advantage to overloading it. They call it supercharging, but it's not worth it. It definitely yielded more power, but not a full day's worth. The only way it could make sense is if I was using rats like a lot of underground collectors. The problem with that is siphoners with enough tech skills could snatch them up and break through the firewalls.

I glance at a dingy solar panel in the old converted alley as I pass it. Most buildings are fitted with solar panels, even along the sides. With the earth's natural resources used up, we have to get power however and wherever we can, never mind the fact that we spend more making some of these panels than they can produce in a decade.

"It has to equal out eventually." That's what people say. In this energy crisis, the goal is akin to perpetual motion:

creating all the power we use. And the most efficient 'machines' aren't machines at all, they are biological: people, animals, things that are alive.

Sure enough, my non-perp tagalong starts jogging too. He must be a siphoner. First off, his flapping trench coat reveals a gaunt frame and no collectors or caps. Only a siphoner would waste energy in hopes to steal some.

I pick up the pace.

I'm in decent shape. In fact, I'm probably in better shape than even high-achieving perps. When my sister, Anise, got diagnosed with Ohm's—a fairly recent disease that seems to be spreading like crazy across the globe—I literally had to step up my output. I doubled my normal routes and even started wearing collectors at home. I plan to get waterproof ones next so I can shower in them. Maybe then, I'd actually bathe a few times a week.

Some people have the luxury to remove their collectors occasionally so they benefit from the extra resistance training all day, and to relax. I've forgotten what it means to relax. If I take any time for myself, I'm taking time off my sister's life, and my mom's.

Every movement counts. I'm saving up for gloves next. If I added finger movement to my daily routes, I could up my output by at least five percent, maybe more. But it would be a month's earning just to cover the gloves, and we don't have the credits to spare. I've already spent most of our savings on these collectors, so I've got to make the most of them.

With Anise fighting the spread of the disease and mom literally on her last leg—amputation sometimes slows the spread—I'm doing all I can to support the three of us.

Anise tries to help. On days she's feeling well enough, I'll put my old collectors on her, but I don't tell her that I've programmed them to a lower rate.

I have to get creative with the tech to convert the power with each update. Mom, on the other hand, can't handle the stress. Even on the lowest settings of our newest models, she struggles, so it's best to leave them off completely for now.

The more present part of me hopes a cure will come along soon, but a deeper part fears the worst. Even if they do, I doubt we could afford the treatment. I barely produce enough for us as is.

If dad was still around, maybe we'd have more power, and more hope. Then again, it'd probably just mean he would have more power. When we finally saved up for him to make the trip to Mecha, we were ecstatic.

This is the dream, to earn enough energy to make it to the holy land of power. When he got back, it was to mean a whole new life for us.

That was two years ago, just as mom got sick. Sometimes I wonder if she told him before he left, but I'd rather not know. He never came back.

If this guy chasing me is a siphoner—and I'm 90% sure he is—then I can't afford to get caught. If he even gets within a few feet of me, he can start leaching my power. And with that siphon tech—the inefficient mobile units—the wireless power collection is terrible. I don't know if I'd be more upset at losing the power or the fact that we'd both be losing around twenty percent of what could be getting at a proper bank. There's nothing worse than wasted energy. I'd almost rather strike a deal with him, but siphoners don't do deals, they just scavenge and even kill for any juice they can squeeze.

I glance at my cap level. It's up to 98.8%. At this rate, I'll be full before I get to the rail station and I'll be wasting power. I decide to take a detour through the nearest park after all. It's better I get partial payment from the giant wireless collector—though only a little more efficient than siphon tech—than lose it outright from this piece of trash chasing me.

Speaking of trash, I jump over another pile of garbage. This trash crisis will probably take us out first. And the higher classes are all worried about having enough power to make their coffee—a luxury I've never afforded, though I hear it can be life-changing.

If I move quickly enough through the park and lose the siphoner, I'll only lose about 25% or so—which is about

10% less than I'd earn at the rail station. I can make that up by sprinting the rest of the way to the rail bank.

As I take the unexpected right turn, the siphoner disappears from the reflections.

He must've taken an earlier alley to cross. I may have lost him.

Part of me thinks about spinning around and heading back toward the rail station. Then I glance down: 99%. I'll be full any minute, and the rest of the walk to the rail bank will be a complete waste. It's still a good ten blocks away or more.

I hesitate but ultimately stick with my plan. Technically, siphoners can't enter the park. Whatever it lacks in efficient transfer, it makes up for in firewalls and safety. I hear not even the latest siphon tech can get through without losing power themselves or setting off an alarm.

There are only a few safe places left in our city where power can't be taken: the trailerhood, because no one has enough power worth taking; the public park banks, where you get bottom cred; and caravan parks when they happen to come through. These are where hopeful people hire safe passage to travel to bigger and better banks.

And most power banks are safe, of course, once you get within a certain distance. You can almost see the radius in the form of stalking siphoners who aren't allowed in public banks.

As greedy as I am for power, it's tear drops in an ocean to a siphoner's greed. They've gone so far as to be ostracized from normal society and the simple freedoms of daily life just so they can have more power and creds to trade in the black market. The only way they can get paid for secondhand power is through the underground markets. Secondhand credits—unless transferred through legitimate means—are tainted and can't be used outside of that market. I'm sure some of them regret it, but there's not much they can do once they cross the line.

Power is taken seriously, and I refuse to let mine be taken at all.

I hear a tiny drone and watch it land on my shoulder while I rush through the alley. I swat it away. That's why they're called swatts. They're all over the city. Originally siphon tech, a lot of them have broken away from their programming and now wander around individually searching for power.

The real threat is when a siphoner has a whole swarm under their control. One or two swatts will barely siphon much power, but if you see a dozen or so, you'd better be worried.

As I burst onto the street, I see the entrance to the park. I jump out of the way of an automated cargo craft. They don't move fast enough to be dangerous, but some ignorant people still get hurt, like I almost just did.

I realize that's my second mistake: stopping again. I don't see him quickly enough to sure my footing, and even though I'm not easy to take down, he tackles me from the right side. We roll together, and I push him away.

"Get off me!"

He's more boy than man, thin with wiry strength and hunger in his eyes. He goes flying, and I almost feel bad for pushing so hard. My sympathy fades quickly when he hops up and smiles.

That can't be good.

I hear a buzzing, and my nightmares come to life. Before I can react, dozens of tiny bug-shaped drones swarm me, some resembling wasps but most like fat beetles with their bulbous, electric blue caps.

I flail uselessly. Even my new firewalls don't stand a chance against this siphon tech. Somehow, they're always an upgrade or two ahead. My only hope is to get to some sort of sanctuary, *like the park.* I sprint toward the gate.

The young man is no longer chasing me. He doesn't have to. Once the swatts get their fill, they'll go right back to the source of their programming code, a little slower and a lot fatter.

I hate to do it but I glanced down at my power meter: *52%?!* if it were just me, I probably wouldn't care as much. Well, I would care, but that 47% I worked so hard for wasn't just for me.

I consider running back to the siphoner to try to beat it out of him, not that it would work. If I cross that line, I wouldn't be any better than him. I would end up in the same place as he is, scrounging for power wherever I can get it. My sister and mother deserve more than that.

And, of course, the power is tainted now, so I couldn't redeem it anyway unless I get involved in places I vowed never to deal with, not since I'd learned what dad really did to get all those filled caps. He was so cranked to think Mecha would honor that hot power.

As I cross through the gate into the park, the swatts detach and swarm back to the alley where the thin boy with black hair and a dirty face once stood.

I glance at my wrist to see I'm down to 30%. That's almost a full day of collecting gone in a matter of seconds. And now I have to use the park-bank, and lose another 10% or more from the inefficiencies and conversion rate I could be getting at the rail station.

It's not too late. If I stay out past curfew again, I can make up some of the loss, but there's no way I can recoup it all. I look at the track, take a deep breath, and start walking.

CHAPTER TWO

I'm an idiot, how could I have let this happen?

The siphoner must've known I was nearly full up based on how I was jogging and where I was headed. All the things I should've done to avoid siphoners seems obvious now. The massive cap-pack is probably the dumbest decision I've made this year, and it's been a terrible year.

The rail station pays more because it's hard-wired which translates to less power loss.

After a wireless collection like the park, however, I know there's some left in the tank; the reader will still show a few percent. To me, a completely empty tank is worth it because I can always fill it up again on my way to a better bank. I guess you could call it potential energy. Anise always laughs at that joke, even if it is a pity-laugh. What irony.

I start jogging to sustain my power and hopefully build it up. The track pulls a little faster than someone can produce at a light jog. A lot of perps will spend all day out here racking up credits, but it's less efficient than hitting up the big banks in my opinion, which take more work and more risk.

The middle of the park tempts me. There are a few courts with a dozen people playing tennis and basketball. Even from this distance, I can see the ball game has gotten competitive. Few, if any, are wearing their collectors. I'd be tempted to take mine off so I could really play, but that's a luxury for future me.

I check my cap level. It hasn't changed from 30%. At this rate, it's an even swap: I'm earning what I'm exchanging.

If I ever get to Mecha though—the biggest bank in what's left of the U. S., near the old Chicago before mass chaos split the country apart—then I could really get top cred. I've been planning a trip, but I can never save up enough power to justify it, not while taking care of mom and Anise. The idea is to buy or rent a cargo craft and join a caravan for protection, but that can't happen anytime soon.

Just outside the park, something familiar catches my eye, or someone. Though there's no longer a swarm, I recognize his raven hair even under the hood. The swarm is dormant, probably hugging his body or discharging power into a cap he may have nearby—my power. Again, I consider pummeling him, but there's no point.

On the next lap, I look for him again. A jogging perp blurs my vision. I look around her to see the strung-out siphoner still staring at me, still waiting.

He wants what's left. Or maybe he's just waiting on the next innocent bystander, but most people who walk out of the park are power-dry. No, he's definitely waiting on me, which means I'm not getting to the power bank after all.

I focus on the blurry figure in my view. It's a girl jogging at my pace—which is impressive. She glances at me out of the corner of her eye, and I turn forward quickly. I realize what it looks like. I wasn't staring at her, well, not at first.

One thing that's inescapable is how beautiful she is. I usually avoid pretty girls because the ones who give someone like me attention are most likely siphoners. I'm not the most attractive guy, but my build works in my favor. Since mom got sick, I've really leaned out with the extra collecting.

All an attractive girl has to do is flirt a little, touch one of my collectors in playful jest, and the siphon tech gets to work on my firewalls. I won't make that mistake again.

I look back at her as if to apologize for staring, though I realize how dumb that is. She raises her eyebrows in a questioning look, only slightly perturbed.

Great, there goes any chance I would've had. Not that I have time for this anyways. Why would I want someone else to care about, to worry about, to protect?

I look down at the cloth strips I've turned into makeshift gloves. A few feet of material wrapped around my hands is a lot cheaper and easier than real gloves. And why would I spend money on simple gloves when I could put that towards collectors?

I realize I look like a creep now, but I also know that anyone who looks like her should be used to the attention.

"Sorry," I say, almost yelling, and not exactly sure why I'm apologizing. "I wasn't looking at you."

We both keep our jogging pace, but I move closer to her, studying her face to see if she's okay with that.

"Not that I wouldn't," I say quickly. "I mean, I would like to look at you, but...not in that way...I was just..."

Maybe shut up. Yeah, that would probably be best.

The corner of her mouth lifts in a smile, forming a dimple like my mother's, one I haven't seen in a long time. I face forward again.

I'm getting tired of not getting paid enough for what I collect. I commit to myself to really consider the Mecha trip, as crazy as it might be. Maybe within a year, if I plan well enough and stay away from siphoners . . . I'll have to ditch this cap-pack though, or get several more to store away until the trip.

"I was afraid you had figured out a new way to siphon power by staring," she says, and I'm surprised she's even talking to me. "The way you were looking, I should be completely drained by now."

She slows down to a walk, and I do the same.

If a girl like this is willing to talk to me, it would be rude to ignore her, right?

When I study her face, I can't help but notice how perfect freckles dot her nose. Sometimes there can be too many freckles. Don't get me wrong, they are beautiful on anyone, but something about this girl just seems...perfect. I wish I had another word.

Somehow, the word slips out, "Perfect." I shake my head and say, "No," I mumble. "I mean, yes, perfect timing. Someone actually is trying to siphon, but it's not me." I nod back toward the boy, and she glances over her shoulder.

"Ugh, I've seen him before. I hate siphoners," she says. "They think they rule the streets, and everyone has to run around in fear. Why can't we just exist together and go our own ways?"

"Exactly," I say, "and actually work for our own power. What a crazy idea." This is a common sentiment, but it's nice to talk to someone other than doctors and bill collectors. I feel attraction growing, but I push it down.

She's just nice, as uncommon as that is, that's all.

I know better anyways. I should, but why wouldn't I see what happens? She can't be a siphoner, not if she's in this park. That sparks a thought to keep us talking.

"If I were a siphoner, could I be in here?" I ask.

"Not unless you were on the cutting edge of siphon tech," she says.

I point my thumb to my outdated cap-pack. "Does it look like it?"

She starts to laugh but stifles it. "I think it's live, very retro."

She really is nice, this can't be real.

"It wouldn't be worth siphoning in here anyways," she says. "Most of us are at work right now, just making enough to keep going."

"Yeah, but they can wait out there all night," I nod to the guy watching us.

"What a waste," she says, looking first at me, then at the boyish man. "You should just sit and let your pack go empty. Then, he'd have no reason to wait."

"I can't do that--sit still, I mean. And I really wanted to take this to the rail bank to get top cred."

"Might as well take it to the holy land," she laughs.

I don't tell her that's my ultimate goal, though it's everyone's goal. Of course, it'll take a lifetime to fill a cargo craft with these old caps.

"Yeah, sure, three months' journey to cash in one cap . . . sounds like a great idea."

"Might be more profitable than dealing with siphoners. You know that thing is literally a target on your back, right?"

Of course I know this now, but had the option of this older model or a smaller, lower capacity model. I had gotten so excited about how cheap it was and how much juice it could carry that I thought it was worth the lack of style.

For a split second, her blue eyes make me think she's full of electricity. I wonder if she's wearing contacts or if she's had her eyes modified. They do seem unnaturally bright, then again, I've learned to avoid anything beautiful.

"You know, I just had that same thought not long ago," I say, "but I can't afford slim-caps. Apparently you can." I eye her up and down once, more for show, but I do notice very few bulges in her clothing, other than the ones that catch my interest naturally. I do my best not to scan her again. I can tell she's waiting for it, and, in the same way, I can also tell she's impressed when I don't break eye contact.

"Sure," she says hesitantly. "Maybe we should know each other's names before we bash each other like old frenemies. I'm Shae," she says with a smile that nearly takes the words out of my mouth.

"Nash," I say, at nearly the same time I hear it in someone else's voice.

The voice enters my head but is absolutely silent to anyone but me due to the cochlear devices just below my ears. Usually, I get an alert or request with such a call, but the fact that it went direct means it's from my inner circle, not that I have many other contacts anyway.

"Nash!" my sister's voice vibrates my skull almost imperceptibly. I start to wince, but the auto-volume function keeps it from hurting. "Something's wrong with mom," she says, her voice breaking but not from the connection. "You need to come home."

"Anise?" I breathe out, but the sound of a disconnected link chimes before I can ask what's going on.

CHAPTER THREE

"Is it Nash or Anise?" She asks with amusement despite my eyes darting around. "Is something wrong?"

I barely hear her question as I bolt toward the nearest exit. I don't care if 'swarm-boy' is out there waiting for me. If he gets in my way, I'll hit him so hard I'll knock the programming out of his siphon tech.

As I rush out, I see his crooked smile.

Just do it, step in front of me, I stare the threat through him.

To my surprise, his gaze drifts away from me, and I'm able to run right by him. Then, I hear my name yelled, and I realize why the swarm isn't on me.

"Nash! Is everything okay?"

Shae must've followed me out. How has she made it this far and remained so decent? And now, because of me, she is that creep's next target.

Siphoners are predators, always choosing the easier mark, though I'm sure her newer tech can work in her favor if needed.

"Get back in the park!" I yell, but it's too late. The swarm has positioned itself between her and the entrance.

I look in the direction of my trailer-hood, then back to Shae. There's no good choice here, and I regret my decision either way, but at least mom isn't alone right now. Besides, I owe that guy some payback.

I sprint back, aiming at the little stick of a man pulling the bug-bot strings. An idea crosses my mind that I hardly ever consider. I access the panel on my wrist that controls my tech and disengage my knee collectors so I can move faster.

He doesn't know what hit him, and based on the six feet he goes flying, he won't remember when he wakes up. I gotta admit, that felt good.

But it doesn't stop the swarm. Once a swatt attaches, the park won't allow that person to enter. Shae must know this as she's already running down the street, swatts all around her.

I spy a service hatch, the kind most people ignore, and come up with a quick, not-so-well-thought-out, plan.

"Over here!" I grab the hatch and pull.

It's stuck. I access my controls again.

Some people have enhanced collectors that can be reversed, drawing on collected power to provide superhuman-like strength or speed.

I don't have such a sophisticated set. I'm all about efficiency, never wanting to spend more energy than I collect. But now, I have to do something I never planned to.

I disengage the rest of my collector functions for minimal resistance. Dropping from the highest earn-setting to nothing makes me feel lighter than air.

My arms float up briefly, and my taut muscles threaten to jerk just as I relax them.

I grab the hatch door again, and I can feel the strength in my arms and legs. I just hope my hands can keep up. If only I had the gloves, I could've been building hand strength as well. The problem now is that my elbow, shoulder, and wrist strength could cause me to break my fingers.

I'm surprised, like I no longer know my limits. The hatch opens slowly, just enough for someone to slip through.

I start to remove my cap-pack, but the opening still isn't big enough.

"Over here!" I shout. Shae runs toward me with the bots still swarming. I realize that it won't help to leave the hatch open and let the swarm follow her in, and it sure won't help for me to be standing here when the swarm does disengage to look for it's next target.

I get down on my knees and pull on the hatch. I can't get it to open any wider. So I lay on my back, grab the opening with my hands, and put my legs on the hatch door. When I push with all my strength, both the rusted hinges and I groan as the hatch opens ninety degrees from the street. All this resistance makes me envy how much energy could have been collected with that effort.

There's no ladder because these access tunnels are not meant to be used by civilians. They're just open holes to the underground network of power banks and building supports, as well as some obsolete and restricted subway tunnels.

I look down into the dark hole with no way to gauge the depth. Then, I look along the street to the path I usually take home. The fear in Anise's voice echoes in my mind, and I wonder if I'm doing the right thing here.

Anyone would forgive me for leaving Shae to fend for herself. Or I could drop my cap-pack in the hole and leave her there until I can come back. Then, the swatts would have no reason to swarm me.

But I obviously can't do that.

I realize the swarm will have no problem following us down if I don't think of some way to stop them, or at least slow them down. Even without their master, they'll siphon until they've had their fill.

I can't believe I'm doing this, I think as I unwrap one of my hands. I tie one end of the cloth rope to my cap sitting next to me.

The hatch is open enough to let Shae past me. She's moving fast, and I see her drop to the ground in a slide like one of those old baseball films. I grab my cap and toss it toward the swatts, hoping my quick knot will hold.

The swarm takes the bait, and she slides into the hole with only a few bugs trailing her. I yank on the rope and my cap flies back to me.

I catch it with one hand and hold the inside of the hatch door with the other as I scoot over the edge, dropping into the hole. My weight is just enough to pull the hatch door shut.

CHAPTER FOUR

Hanging from the hatch door, I once again curse myself for upgrading my collectors instead of getting the gloves. My hands are already screaming for relief.

Looking up, I see some glowing residue and a few sparks from smashed swatts.

"Is it clear down there?" I ask. I don't remember hearing Shae hit the ground, but I was a little busy. Glancing down, I see about half a dozen flying lights, vampiric fireflies, easy enough to deal with.

"Yeah," she says from a spot out of the way. I'm surprised at how relieved I am to hear her reply.

I let go of the hatch handle and fall a few feet. I recognize the distance as the same as letting go of the rim on a basketball goal.

I allow my legs through recoil to catch my weight. Then I open my wrist panel again to turn on collection again, but I'm not wearing my cap. It won't hurt to have it on, but if I try to plug my cap in while the collectors are on, I could get quite the jolt from the open connection.

I put in on and connect the cables. Then I engage my collectors again.

What am I doing? I think as I realized I haven't even checked on Shae.

"Are you okay?" I say as I hunch by her side.

"You sure need those creds, huh?" she says, and I feel some of her remorse for what she's gotten us into. "Sorry," she catches herself. "You didn't have to help me like that. I'm fine, I flipped my collectors when I saw the swatts coming. I'd rather use up my power than give it up."

That explains how she moved so fast and landed from ten feet up without a sound. Also, she's not wearing a large cap like my own, which I finally decide for sure is not worth the trouble.

"How much did they get?" I ask.

"Basically the rest of what I had," she says and adds, "but I didn't have much after the park."

I watch her eye as it's trained on a glowing swatt. Then, nearly as fast as a lighting arc, she grabs it from the air.

There's a barely audible sound from the crunch, and she turns her hand over and opens it. The gel-like substance that houses the energy is smeared across her palm along with bits of aluminum and polycarbonate.

"That's strange," she says, not looking at her hand.

I follow her gaze to see the other few swatts moving together, away from us. Why wouldn't they be after our energy? Without programming, they automatically go after the largest energy source, which should be my cap, which should be around 34% right now.

"Maybe they know a way out?" I say without thinking, realizing we might be trapped in here ourselves. I know I could jump up to the hatch door again if I need to, but as hard as it was to open the hatch from above, I don't see how I could from below.

"We both know they don't care about that. They just want power."

The only sources of light are from our collectors and caps, and hers shine through some parts of her clothing. Tracing them, I can see she has some of the most slim-line collectors I've seen, not even available on the market yet, maybe the black market?

I also noticed earlier that she doesn't have a large cap or backpack. She might even have a full body suit. That could mean a few things, either she comes from a wealthy family—which isn't likely if she's hanging out at my local power bank park—or she's well connected in another way. It's also possible that she's like me, someone who came from nothing and worked hard to earn the next highest tech.

If I avoided siphoners and didn't have to take care of my family, I could probably earn enough at my current productive rate to do the same.

Anise! Mom! How could I forget?

I've got to get home. I have to know what's wrong. I try to call Anise, but I can't get signal. Must be from being in this room underground.

"I really need to get out of here," I say, trying to see anything but the darkness. My eyes are slowly adjusting.

"Me too," she says, already following the last swatt. The others have squeezed through a loose panel in a wall.

We watch the last bot go through the small gap, light still emanating from the small space.

I press my face up against it, but can't see through. As I back up, the entire wall illuminates. I turn around and have to shield my eyes from the energy efficient LEDs in Shae's headband. Another upgrade I never thought worth it.

"They're probably just crawling away," she says, "looking for the park's power core or something."

"Maybe, but my bet is with them unless you have a better plan, which I assume you don't." I realize how harsh my words sound, but I'm not focused on protecting her right anymore. She's safe because of me, and because of that, I'm stuck here instead of home helping my sister.

"I'm sorry," Shae says, surprising me. I expected a harsh retort to match mine, but her voice is sincere. "You didn't have to help me like that. Thank you."

I feel her hand on my shoulder, and I jerk myself away out of instinct. Most women who try to touch me are after my power.

"Sorry," I say. "I'm just not used to, well, you know, with all the siphoners out there, I have a hard time trusting people anymore. I know you're not--" but I stop myself as I realize I may have read her wrong.

I glance at my power rating again. It's down to 32%, but it shouldn't be dropping. I back away.

Considering the tech level of her suit, it's possible she could be a professional siphoner, but again, why would she be in this back-alley neighborhood?

"Don't worry, I'm not what you think I am, and I know you're not either, or else you wouldn't have helped me like you did, especially while you were in such a hurry. That means even more. Do you mind if I ask what's wrong? How can I help?"

I want to believe her, but all of this makes more sense to think she's after my power. But anyone can tell I don't have much, so it would be a waste of time, wouldn't it?

She drops her head, then her light flashes across my face as her eyes come up to meet mine. There's that word again floating in my mind, the one that describes her electric eyes and symmetric face. I allow myself to get lost in it for a moment this time.

No, don't fall for it, not again.

"I guess I'm trying to say, 'thank you,' but that's not enough. I wish I could give you what power I have left, though it's not much. I would've lost it anyways."

Power used to be easy to exchange willingly, but then people started getting mugged for power, forced at gunpoint to transfer. When energy started getting controlled and caps automatically marking it for one-way transfers, that's when siphoning really exploded.

Part of me wonders if there's a way to transfer without altering the energy signature, but I couldn't take anything from his girl even if I wanted to. She's already taken something from me, and I'm trying to guard myself from more.

"I just want to get home so I can help my sister."

"Is that Anise?" Shae asks.

I turn around quickly to look at her as I realize how she knows my sister's name. I must've said it back at the park.

"Yes, our mom is sick. So is Anise, but she called and said it's an emergency, something's wrong with Mom."

"Oh no," Shae's eyes widen before she looks down and away. "And you're not there because you're stuck here with me." Tears start to pool. "This is my fault."

I want to say it's not, but I can't quite believe those words just yet. If the blame goes anywhere, it falls on me.

Then, she pushes past me as she makes an adjustment on her own wrist regulator. She grabs the loose panel and rips it away from the wall. As dark as it is on this side, any amount of light is helpful, but this is more than I expect. The faint glow that was coming through is now as bright as Shae's headlamp, brighter actually.

"You go through there and start looking for a way out," she says. "I'll use my light to check around on this side. Let's meet back in--" she eyes her wrist, "three minutes."

I nod and turn toward the room. As impressed as I am with Shae's leadership, I'm more curious about this glow. It was getting dark outside, and with the energy curfews, it's a bad idea to be out there at that time. I'd be better off sleeping in the park or maybe walking all night. Of course, that's not an option. I have to get home.

This means the light in this room isn't natural. I squat down, the space just large enough for me--once I take off my cap-pack--and start to crawl through. I do notice that my cap is starting to glow a bit more. Last I checked, it was around 30%, so it shouldn't be too bright. If I had the higher end models, the outer linings would hide the contents better, though not completely, like Shae's.

I feel a slight physical reaction. It could be adrenaline, but I feel good, like it's easier to move and that nagging headache that's usually there from overexertion is nearly gone. Then, I remember that my collectors are turned off, and I haven't been doing much for the last few minutes. Still, I haven't felt anything like this before.

This space continues on and I realize it's a tunnel, not just a wall to another room. I crawl toward the bright light on the other side. I can't see much else yet.

As I approach the end, the room becomes visible. I can't believe what I'm seeing. This explains the light too. It's a supercharged—or super-filled, depending on who you ask —capacitor. These are rare. As a cap, it's nothing special, but the fact that it has been continuously overcharging for who-knows-how-long, makes it extremely valuable.

When I exit the tunnel, I don't even look around the room. I start to study the cap. I can't find any cables running into it and wonder how it could stay supercharged without an influx of power. The cap is nearly the size of mine—which oddly enough seems to be glowing brighter than before.

I glance at the more illuminated supercharged cap. It must be twice what my cap holds or more. Most people don't have the patience or resources to supercharge their caps. I've heard of entire farms full of them, but I doubt they make as much money after keeping power flowing in and siphoners finding their ways in. Then again, with a labor force on the grounds 'voluntarily' discharging their power for pay—which is frowned upon by the designers and makers—the exchange rate could make it more profitable.

This, however, is no farm. It's an abandoned room under a park-bank. I finally look around and nearly fall over when I see what I've truly stumbled into. The room is like a small warehouse, and I can see every corner. There are dozens of supercharged caps—possibly over hundred—down here as well as plenty of swatts and scavenger bots, but they're all supercharged as well, so satiated with power they can't even move, serving simply as night-lights for me.

I'm tempted to hook up to it, but that's too dangerous with my tech. I know this all too well. Maybe Shae's newer tech can read it, but I don't think I'd want to be around if she did.

These are highly unstable—another risk in using them. I remember a neighbor's trailer completely exploding because they tried to over-fill a small cap to see what would happen. They were using siphon tech they shouldn't have had. It was sad too, because they put a lot of their resources and power into it. Looking back, I should've learned from that, not to use a single cap but to spread out the investments.

Instead, I put my cap-pack back on and am even more confused when I see the reading: 34%. There's no way I built up a few percent in a matter of minutes. That's at least an hour of intense activity. Thinking back to when it read less and now more, I wonder if my cap is messing up, but I'm coming up with a different theory now.

Is it possible...? I start to wonder. Then I imagine how much money I could get for these. I could make the Mecha trip.

This is what I've been waiting for—well, not exactly. It's not like I knew this kind of place existed. I doubt anyone knows or it would be exploited like everything else.

Part of me perks up when I remember Shae, excited to share something so momentous. Then, I consider not telling her. The reason we're here is because of me actually, not her. I chose to help her, I found the hatch, and I followed the bots to this room. If I don't tell her, nothing in her life will change.

Nothing in her life will change . . . but if I do tell her, she will have the chance to rise out of this life.

There's also the possibility that I might want to spend more time with her. If that's true, then starting a friendship with a lie—especially one this big—could cause some real problems. More than that though, I'm swayed by my moral responsibility to help a fellow perp who's just trying to make a better life for herself.

Before I decide for sure, I hear her voice echo through the tunnel.

"Hey, Nash! I found a way out!"

This is my chance, it's time to choose. As much power as there is in here, we can both have more than enough.

"Shae!" I close my eyes. This will change everything, for better or worse. "You've got to see this."

CHAPTER FIVE

"I found a way out . . . holy juice," Shae says when she makes it through the tunnel. "What is this place?"

"I don't know, but I think we're the only ones who know about it. Can you keep it between us?"

"Um, yes. What about you?"

"I will. I'll have to find a way to explain it to my mother and sister somehow."

"I'm sure they won't complain when life gets better for them. We'll have to get creative on the best way to cash these things in. The banks will know something's up if we bring too many at once."

I consider telling her my plan, but I wait until I hear her out.

"That's true," I say. "We have to take them to the rail station, at least. Only the bigger banks can handle supercharged caps."

Shae nods and looks down at her wrist. She bumps it with her other hand. "This thing hasn't worked right since we got down here. I think the swatts messed it up."

"Let me guess, it's reading high."

"Yeah, how'd you know?"

I point to my wrist. "Mine too. There might be more happening down here than we think. I'm not sure if it's even possible, but I think our caps are being charged by something around us, just like these caps and all the swatts."

Shae looks around, then back to the tunnel, then above her.

"We're under the park," she says. "They always talk about how inefficient these parks are, but they're so convenient. Maybe they're leaking power and all these things are soaking it up."

That's the same theory I've been contemplating, and I think she's right.

"That would explain a lot," I say. "How about your body?" I ask before thinking and scan her frame. Despite the slimline collectors and caps, I can tell she has a nice figure. It's the curse of some men to see more than we're supposed to. Of course, most active perps are in good shape.

I look away as I realize what it looks like and try to cover. "Are you feeling any...different?"

"I am actually, almost like I turned my collectors off, even though I haven't. That's why I thought they were malfunctioning."

"Exactly!" I say. "We'll have to come back soon to figure this out, but I can't stay any longer." I grab one of the supercharged caps on my way back to the tunnel.

When Shae raises an eyebrow, I say, "Might as well take one while we can. Besides, I'm curious how much is in one of these things."

I'm surprised--though I shouldn't be--when I go to lift the cap to find it's heavier than any I've ever moved before. Unfortunately, I can't discharge this juice at home, unless I want to risk an explosion like my neighbor.

She shrugs and grabs two. I would have as well except for the fact that I have to carry mine out also, and the tunnel won't allow me to wear it.

"Don't you want to take inventory or something?" she asks.

"I can't waste any more time. My mom needs me."

"Yeah, sorry. Maybe I could stay here and do it then?"

Something inside me doesn't like the way she offers that, and I certainly don't like thinking about the possibilities here. This just got a lot more complicated. Once again, I chide myself for making the wrong choice. Next time I find a veritable gold mine of power, I'm keeping it to myself. She would've understood eventually, assuming anything came out of our relationship.

She must be able to read the feelings on my face because she says, "Don't worry. I'll be fair. We can split it down the middle, and I'll only take these tanks tonight. I guess we need to make some kind of agreement. We kind of barely know each other."

I feel time passing and think about my sister at home dealing with whatever's going on.

"No," I say tersely. "Sorry, I just don't have time for this. Let's both leave now, and we'll come back here tomorrow, first thing. Let's say six? If we can trust each other enough to do that, then I'll know I can work with you."

"And I with you," she adds, then stares longingly at the room as I squat down to enter the tunnel. I do wonder if she'll try to come back in the middle of the night, but I've got a plan for that already. As for now, I need to find a way to seal the room so that only two of us can open it.

If she's smart, she won't involve anyone else in this, and she should know it will take more than one night to clear this place, even with help. That's also assuming she has a place to store her volatile caps.

As I crawl through the tunnel, I dream of the Mecha trip. With just two supercharged caps, I could probably buy a cargo craft and pay to join a caravan. I think about offering to do this together, but it's too soon to bring it up.

Once I get out of the tunnel, I reconnect my cap-pack and start looking for something large enough to cover the panel. The supercharged cap lights up the space, and when Shae crawls out, she only has one cap, but it illuminates the rest of the small maintenance area.

"Where's the other one?" I ask.

"I figured it'd be a little conspicuous to be seen carrying two supercharged caps through the city, especially at night."

She pulls something from her pocket and shakes it out. It's a bag that she uses to cover the cap. It does a decent job of hiding the glow.

"Got another one of those?" I ask.

"If I did, I would've brought the other cap." She smiles, and I reciprocate. It feels good for a moment until I remember why I'm in a hurry.

My lips flatten and I continue my search. "Help me find something big."

She doesn't even have to ask why. She turns on her headlight, and we start looking for something to cover the tunnel.

I find a large metal bin--a discarded tool of some sort--maybe a concrete mixer? When I try to move it, it doesn't budge. I take note of a few concrete bags next to it.

"This might work," I say, and Shae comes to help. Even with my collectors disengaged and hers flipped, we struggle to move it. Every few inches we scoot it, I'm beating myself up for not just leaving. I question myself. *Am I letting greed and distrust outweigh my family's need?*

I decide that protecting this vault is actually *for* my family, and it encourages me to push harder. After too many minutes, the mixer—still filled with hardened concrete, which is probably why they left it—is blocking the panel as if it was there the whole time.

I jog back over to the concrete bags and start to rip one open. They concrete has long-since hardened from exposure to water, but the bags are dried enough to rip off easily. I grab enough to wrap the cap. As odd as it may look, carrying concrete will get less attention than the world's largest nightlight.

If they got all that stuff down here, there must be a larger access door.

"Did you say you found another way out?" I ask.

"Yeah, follow me."

I appreciate her hastiness. A terrible feeling starts filling my stomach as I finally consider the possibilities.

When we try to get onto the street, I understand why this maintenance shaft isn't used often. We have to push a dumpster aside and wade through dozens of bags of trash.

As soon as we get into the alley, notifications flood into my cochlear device and wrist control.

"Ten missed voice messages from: 'Home'. Twenty-two written messages from: Sis."

I'm still overwhelmed by the smell and the mushy consistency in the bags. This stuff has been here for a long time and will probably stay for a good while. Of course, the refuse overload is second only to the energy crisis.

I take off running before Shae even makes it out.

The last message from Anise reads, "I hope what you were doing was important. Mom is gone."

I don't even say goodbye to Shae. I already missed the goodbye that mattered most.

CHAPTER SIX_

I stand at the hatch again, holding my sister's hand and waiting for Shae. It's been a week since mom passed. Anise is still a little upset with me but mostly upset that our mother is gone. I didn't even try to explain myself for the first few days. We were so busy getting things ready for the cremation.

It was a simple memorial held in our home. I was able to use the supercharged cap to get enough funds for the service, even though we kept it simple. It really just helped pay for the mandatory cremation. If you can't pay, they pull from your future credits until it's covered. Clearly, that pushes a lot of people to underground market and siphoning.

The hardest part of the evening when mom passed was leaving Anise alone again. I knew she wouldn't sleep that night, so I couldn't sneak off. I didn't want her to carry the burden of what I'd find, so I just told her I need to go to the park again, to run out my frustration and earn some more credits for . . . well, for the funeral, but I didn't say that.

What I really did was keep a lookout for Shae and anyone she might have recruited to rob the power mine.

Just as I'd suspected, I ran into Shae, but she was alone. It turned out she was doing the same thing. The fact that we didn't trust each other actually proved to each other that we aren't idiots. It added to our strange bond.

I told her what happened, and she said she could wait a week to go back down, even though her excitement was evident by her excess energy.

We decided to run anyways, and I probably filled half a tank that night on top of what the park converted. Something about being with Shae helped my pain fade away for awhile. It could have to do with our shared secret and all the potential down there, but that didn't matter to me as much now that mom is gone.

I still need to care for Anise, but I've heard of new experimental treatments for Ohm's. Now that we have a way to get the funds, I'll be able to take her to the best doctors.

It's been amazing to spend those nights with Shae without feeling pressure to go to the power mine. We occasionally pop open the access hatch in the road to make sure the concrete mixer hasn't been moved, but she never pushes me to go down there. I'm actually starting to trust her.

Honestly, despite the nightly runs and talks, I haven't learned much about her. We don't even talk about what we'll do with our cuts after we get top cred. I don't have big plans, other than helping Anise, and maybe moving out of this place. There aren't many places out there much better. I could use my wealth to become an aristo, but that would mean I would need to keep the money coming. Apparently, even a fortune doesn't last long at that level. That may be possible though, if other power parks are like ours.

What I really want though is to get a farm, though it's not what it sounds like. Those used to be where some of the most impoverished people lived off the land. Now, they are mostly self-sustaining plots, though they only use what they produce.

I put a down payment on a cargo craft—nothing too flashy, but one that will hold and protect plenty of supercharged caps safely. The nearest caravan park is about three miles outside of the city. As long as I can get in their radius, I'll be safe for long enough to hire real protection. They have unofficial laws governing their mobile parks, but they aren't always around.

As hard as it is to think this way, it's better that mom is gone. With enough supplies, Anise can take care of herself. She's not stable enough to come with me. I am actually going to make the Mecha trip. Every time I think about it, I still can't believe it.

Shae wants to send most of her portion with me in order to get the best return. I haven't invited her to join me yet. I'm still thinking about it, wondering if it might be better for her to be around in case Anise needs help.

Also, Shae has some lofty plans, though she won't tell me much about them. However, she's going to use some of it right away for something she isn't ready to tell me about. Based on our conversations, my guess is that she will help others escape a life of siphoning by covering some of their bills. I wish I was that selfless, but my main concern is Anise.

One thing we haven't talked much about is the weird, amped up feeling we both got while in that room. Soon enough, we'll know if my other theory has any merit.

"Hey, stranger," I hear her familiar honey tone behind me, " . . . and stranger's sister."

"I'm Anise," my sister says, greeting Shae with skepticism in her eyes. "So, you're the reason my brother has been so...busy."

I can see that Shae understands why Anise is skeptical. "I suppose so. It's great to meet you, Anise, I'm Shae. And I know you're tired of hearing this, but I'm so sorry to hear about...well, everything. I was with your brother when it happened, and, though it doesn't fix anything, I promise it will make some sense soon."

"Nothing makes sense anymore," Anise says.

I understand that, it's how I felt when dad never showed up again. But she's too young to have those feelings . . . right? I guess I was close to her age then. She's always been the happy one, the one everyone likes. I've been the brooding, disinterested loner. The fact that she's showing this side of herself to someone she barely knows must mean she's really losing hope. I've been to that point, so I know she's reaching out, maybe for the last time.

"I know what you mean," Shae says. "I actually don't have any family, not anymore, not really. Most of them got pulled into siphoning, some were tricked, some were forced, and some just had enough of our twisted and controlling society."

It's crazy how the last two women in my life just met but they're already opening up like neither has to me. This is all enlightening to me, and it means my intuition has been fairly good so far.

"How about we get where we're going, before anyone notices?" I suggest as I hold my hand out for her.

"*Please,*" Anise elongates. "It's freezing and it stinks and I don't want to be out here."

"Are you feeling okay?" I say, the overprotective brother coming out. "If you need to, we can try this another time."

"No, I'm fine," she says, rolling her eyes. "I mean, I'm not amazing or anything--not that I've felt that way in a while--but I can manage a little while longer...as long as you don't keep wasting time checking on me." She raises an eyebrow, but I know her well enough to sense her appreciation for my affection.

Shae leans her head toward Anise for a moment. "I like her," she whispers, adding a smile, then steps over a bag of mushy garbage.

"Let me carry you," I offer with my arms out.

"I can walk," Anise argues, then looks down. "But maybe after we get past this trash?"

I forget how light she's become due to the degeneration. Usually, I keep the collectors on the highest settings to convert more energy, so now when I hold her weight, I sense what a stick she's become.

She accepts, and I follow Shae through the garbage path we've carefully left in place. If we create a trail, someone will eventually wander into it.

When we reach the dumpster, Shae puts one hand against the brick building and pries the dumpster away with the help of her collectors. I don't know how she had the time, but she upgraded again. I can barely see the caps or collectors through her clothes, and I've been checking.

I finally got the gloves and a slimmer cap, but I'm being careful not to spend too much for obvious reasons. Siphoners aren't always smart, but there are some who can almost smell power, and they're great at picking up a scent. That's why I worry about Shae. I hope she's buying a little at a time from various places and covering her tracks.

I set Anise down so she can squeeze past the dumpster. I follow and try to pull it shut. It doesn't budge. I've never been able to close it myself, but I always try.

Shae reaches a superpowered arm out and we pull it together.

"Where are we?" Anise asks. "And why in the middle of the night?"

"You'll see soon enough," I assure her. "And we can't risk being followed."

Shae and I walk up to the mixer and begin to push. With Shae's newest enhancements, it's a lot easier to move this time. I wonder if she could do it herself actually, which sparks my distrustful side a moment. I try to bed it down but also try to remember exactly how the room looked before.

"Wow, what is that?" Anise asks, peering at the light coming through the tunnel.

"Wait til you get to the other side," Shae says through her smile.

I lead the way in case something is waiting on us, though Shae is the most formidable among us. Also, I need to see if the room looks the same as I remember. I really like Shae, but deception is one thing I can't forgive.

Anise follows me, and once we are in the power mine, I turn around to watch her face.

What I see makes last week's suffering almost worth it. Anise is smiling. I can actually see her teeth without her taking a bite of something.

And not only that, I can also see a new glow on her. Of course the light from all the supercharged caps is playing a part, but there's something else.

She is standing almost completely straight up for the first time in a long time. Ever since the degenerative disease-- which we think is caused by early generation collectors-- took root in her, she had started to shrink in many ways. Mom, who had it longer, went from nearly 6 feet tall to barely able to stand to five and half feet in a matter of months.

Anise has only been sick for a few months herself and has never stood like this since getting sick.

This is what I hoped would happen. Something about this room is helping her. I can't believe it, but I also can't believe how all of these capacitors are getting supercharged when they aren't hooked up to collectors.

Honestly, I don't care at this point. Just seeing my sister smile and move like she hasn't in months is all I could ever ask for. And she notices it too.

"I don't know what's happening," she says, "but I feel amazing."

She looks around at all the caps, then stares hard at me.

"This is why you brought me here," she says. I look past her as Shea climbs through the tunnel and stands up.

"That was fast," she says, staring at my sister.

"What do you mean?" I ask, my tone a little too suspicious.

"You know what I'm talking about," she says with a slight eyebrow raise. "We both knew there was something strange about this place, almost healing, and I'm pretty sure this is why you brought your sister here."

Of course she knows, I think. She probably had the idea the same time I did if not before. I don't know why I keep underestimating this girl's intelligence and foresight. I guess it's because I want to trust her. And if I keep myself suspicious, always looking for something, then I can't grow close to her like I want.

"I just wasn't sure," I said. "But yeah, I had a feeling--and not just physically when I walked in the first time--but I had this hope. If only we found this place a day earlier..."

"Don't say that, brother. The past is behind us, and we can only move in one direction if we want to survive, or even rise above it." My sister squats. I see what she's trying to do, and I try to stop her, but it's too late.

She pushes up, and her feet leave the ground. When she lands, she crumples to her knees, and I rush to her side.

"What are you thinking?" I say. "Are you okay?"

When she looks up at me, I don't see the expected look of pain but rather a brilliant smile across her face. She laughs. A real laugh that spreads into my own chest until I can't hold back mine.

We laugh together. It's the most wonderful moment, and Anise has never been more beautiful. A joy comes alive in me that hasn't in so long. I see her eyes sparkle and find myself crying as well. We're crying because we're finding ourselves again and mourning the losses of self and more.

"Don't do that again," I say, but this time I'm smiling. "But seriously, you'll need some time to build your strength up. We don't know how this works yet, but you might be like a cap, soaking up the power--the life force-- around you. If that's the case, you'll want to store as much as you can while you can."

I look over at Shae, and her lips move to the side in a thinking gesture. "That's actually not a bad theory, Nash. I think you're onto something, but I don't know if it as limited as you think. The only way to know is by letting her spend some time down here, then going back topside."

"That works for us," I say. "We've got a lot to inventory anyways." I turn to Anise. "Just keep letting me know how you're feeling or if anything does it feel right. We can stay down here until you're—" I look around at all the capacitors and smile when the perfect word comes to me, "supercharged."

CHAPTER SEVEN

When we've got as good a count as we can, we decide to head out. I want Anise to be careful, but if she can carry a cap, that will help. With the three of us working together in different locations, we could cash in pretty quickly.

Based on what I got for the first supercharged cap last week, and the number of similar ones we've found, I can barely fathom the amount of money we'll have after the Mecha trip. In fact, I could just exchange it within our region and the next, even though the nearest country within the former United States territory is in civil war. Since the energy crisis, that's all we hear about, civil wars inside countries that seceded. Looking back, I wonder if the United States wasn't so bad if it managed to hold itself together so long.

Caps aren't the only things either. I haven't even counted the swatts and rodents. Those alone could power our entire trailerhood for a solid month or more—which is what I plan to do with them, without telling anyone, of course. The hood has been good to us for the most part, and when we had mom's wake, they really came together. I just have to figure out how to transfer their power without using the underground market.

The hardest part of all this is going to be keeping this place secret until we know it works. I'll also be bringing as many old caps as I can find. Of those we've found down here, there doesn't seem to be a limitation on which can hold power. Some even go back to the first generation of caps, discarded in the local sewers and park dump because of their inefficiencies. Being supercharged, it doesn't matter now.

I've parked the cargo craft in the trash alley. Shae and I make a plan to load the caps. She insists on going topside first to make sure no one will see what we're up to.

As late as it is, there's always the chance some siphoners are roaming the streets for helpless perps like us..

"I'm not sure about her," Anise whispers to me from inside the tunnel as Shae goes topside.

"What do you mean? I think she's kind of amazing."

"Of course you do. She's something alright. I thought you always told me not to trust a pretty face. If that's the case, you should've run away as fast as possible."

A week ago, that was my first urge when I saw Shae, but I've grown to know her this week.

"She's different," I defend.

"Sure, and I'm in perfect health," Anise jokes. "I'm just saying, anyone who looks like her is hardly ever telling you the whole truth. And what about that story about her family being siphoners?"

"That's not what she said," I say before thinking about it. It is strange that she told Anise those things right away but not me after a full week of time together.

"You aren't taking her with you, are you?" Anise asks.

I turn back to her. She's always had this crazy intuition, something mom and I missed out on.

"I've been thinking about asking her to come, why not? You've got a few people who can check in on you."

"I'll be fine without her, I just don't know about you. Who says she won't turn on you?"

"She hasn't yet, and she's had a week's worth of chances to."

"I still don't trust her," Anise says, and I hate that part of me agrees with her. What else can I do at this point though? I'll just have to watch her close and have a backup plan in case things go wrong.

"All clear!" Shae yells back. "Let's load up!"

"Yes it is," Anise whispers. "Just be careful, big brother."

As I take the first two caps up the stairs, Anise says she's feeling good enough to help, but I warn her again to take it easy. She settles for transporting caps from the room into the tunnel. Then, I grab them and carry them up the stairway to the alley entrance where Shae loads them into the cargo craft.

When we get nearly full, Shae tells us to hold off.

"Go ahead and bag up some bots," she yells down. "I'll make some room."

"Alright, give us a few minutes," I reply.

"Take your time, I really didn't think this through when loading."

I question Shae's methods and the fact that she always seems to think things through, but I'm too excited about the haul. I return to the mine with Anise, and we start collecting the bloated swatts and rodents that are too saturated to move. I look around at the rest of the caps.

I need another cargo craft, I think. Based on the how many we took for this first load, we could make at least four more trips.

I set one of the bags near the tunnel and hear some movement just on the other side. My heart jumps, and I motion to Anise to be quiet as I drop to my knees. I peer through to see a familiar pair of boots.

"Done already? We're about to come through," I say.

Instead of the expected remark, I see the boots light up, which means she's turned on the assisted lift control. The screech of metal against concrete echoes through the tunnel.

"What's going on?" I ask as I start to crawl through. I can't move fast enough as I barely fit as is. I won't make it by the time it closes.

"I'm sorry," I hear her say between grunts and screeching. "I don't have a choice."

"You always have a choice," I hear myself say, recognizing mom's words coming through.

She doesn't answer. She doesn't have to. Against my better judgement, I try to think of what could have happened, but my heart knows the truth. All the little things she's said and done—as well as what she hasn't said or done—come back to me. Anise's warning was right on, and once again, I hate myself for my many should and shouldn't-have decisions.

"What's going on?" Anise asks quietly from the room behind me.

I keep crawling until I reach the panel. I push, but it doesn't budge. There's no more sound coming from the other side. The mixer has us blocked in, and Shae is gone. I try again, my collectors still disengaged, but I know it's a waste of time. I regret not upgrading when I could, but I knew that could bring a lot of attention to someone like me, someone who barely scrapes up the creds for each upgrade.

I look between my knees and down the tunnel to Anise.

"Something's wrong," I say just loud enough for her to hear.

Going backward in the tunnel is ten times as grueling. Time is taken from me, but it doesn't matter now. We're stuck down here until Shae decides she needs another haul, which could be hours or months.

CHAPTER EIGHT

"I'm sorry," Anise says when I finally escape the hell-hole. "I hoped I was wrong."

Me too.

"What do we do now?"

"I have no idea."

If Anise were stronger, and if we could somehow get enough leverage, we could move the mixer, but I know how much it weighs and what it takes. We're trapped, and there's no way around it. If there were a way out, I'm sure the swatts would've found it. Then again, why would they want to leave? This is exactly what they're programmed to find, a rich source of power.

I stare at the supercharged caps, thinking about the entire cargo craft load that Shae is stealing right now. Well, she's only stealing half of it, but that's still an awful thing to do to a friend.

A friend? I was never her friend. I was a mark, and she is a siphoner of the worst kind, the kind that doesn't lurk in corners. At least those kinds of siphoners are honest about who they are.

I really thought I could trust her. I should've listened to my gut all along.

Her tech alone should've tipped me off. She's either a high-level siphoner or she has connections to siphon leaders. Maybe she works for them. They need people with legitimate credentials for a lot of their scams...like being able to walk through a park bank in broad daylight or running into a swarm of swatts without losing much energy so she could build a relationship with someone like me, a high-performing perp who could be valuable in many ways.

Of course, she hit the motherload when we discovered this mine. Now, she's gonna bring her boss here or some thugs to do the dirty work of collecting the rest of the caps and disposing of us.

I look at my sister's big green eyes, the ones we both got from mom, and see the blue from the caps reflecting in them. I see sorrow and admiration, and despite everything, hope.

I can't give up yet. If I can get out of here within the next ten minutes, I can catch her. She'll have to keep it slow with so many combustible caps.

Combustible...

"Anise," I say. "I think I have a terrible idea."

"I don't know if you ever have good ideas." She motions around.

"Look for anything that can shield us from a blast."

"A what? What are you talking about? How are you going to..." She stops when she catches on. "No, no no no, that's insane. You remember that big hole in the ground in our neighborhood?"

"Where do you think I got the idea? Come on, we don't have much time. We'll need to cover the tunnel's opening so the explosion doesn't ignite the rest of the caps. Let's start by moving everything to that corner." I motion to the area farthest from the tunnel. "We'll post up over there," I point to the wall that shares the tunnel opening. "It's the safest place if the fire needs to find a way out."

"That could kill us, Nash."

"Sis, we only have a few choices, and most have to do with how we're going to die. We can suffocate or starve, we can wait until Shae's shady friends find us and kill us or enslave us, or we can fight. And I know you're a fighter, so let's get to work."

Through all the emotions coming across her face, I finally see the one I've been waiting for, and as always, it's accompanied by an eye roll. She starts moving things, but I watch her closely to make sure she isn't overworking herself. There's no way to get help down here, not yet.

We find enough scrap metal and discarded trash to seal up one end of the tunnel.

Of course, we put several swollen swatts around the panel where the mixer is blocking it in. Then, we put one of my new slim-caps at the center. It's the only one we have access to that isn't fully charged.

Then, we carefully attach some loose wires to the swatts.

If it all goes well--meaning the transaction is a total failure, as planned-- the tunnel will act like the chamber of a gun, blowing the mixer out of the way. It will also-- probably--blow debris back into this room, but hopefully not enough to agitate all the other caps.

To be safe, we move most of the caps to the far side of the room, some behind large support posts.

Anise has become quite clever in using remote functions from caps and collectors. It came in handy when mom needed something and neither of them felt up for it, as simple as opening doors or tossing things across the house.

She links to the swatt bundle to my wrist control so that we can set up a wireless transfer of power. Based on what we know, there's only one way to properly discharge a supercharged cap, and this isn't it.

It's already been over ten minutes, but I can move pretty fast once I get out. We don't allow ourselves time to talk ourselves out of this.

"Are you ready?" I ask.

Anise's eyes are wide as she responds. "I don't think either of us are ready for this."

As I close my eyes to wish for success, I feel Anise grab my wrist. I open my eyes to see that she has just pressed the transfer execution on my wrist control. I surround her and put my back to one of the supports, hopefully outside of the blast area, but nothing happens.

"Are you sure we did it right?" I'm not sure why I'm whispering.

Then, as if the room was tossed out of an airplane and finally found the ground, everything shakes with a tremendous, deafening shockwave. My heart stops for a few seconds, and I can't breathe. I squeeze Anise closer and keep my eyes closed.

When I open them, I can barely see anything through all the dust and debris, and I only hear a high-pitched whining noise, the solid drone of sudden tinnitus.

I immediately start coughing but waste no time. I try to pick Anise up, but she pushes me away. She can move fine without me, so we head to the tunnel's opening.

Not only is it wide open, but it's larger than before. I imagine the mixer is cleared, but we'll have to crawl through to know for sure. I glance back to see glowing tubes in the corner and know we're safe for now.

"Grab some caps," I say, but I don't even hear my own voice. Anise mouths something as well but I still hear the ringing. I point to the caps, and we both grab a few, as well as some of the bags of bots.

After that explosion, it's not likely this place will stay secret much longer. Even if it does, we'll need to recoup whatever we can if I don't catch Shae.

As I walk now through the tunnel, still ducking, but able to stay on my feet, I'm glad I don't have to touch the glowing floor or walls. Even through my shoes, I can feel the heat and see molten slag around.

Sure enough, when we reach the tunnel's end, it's wide open. When I locate the mixer—or what's left of it—I really get a sense of the power inside these caps. That was just a handful of swatts. I can't imagine what one the size of my cap-pack would do. Well, I've seen what it can do, and there's a crater in the trailer-hood to prove it.

Despite the fact that I'm leaving this treasure trove vulnerable, I have one goal right now. I know every bank within a hundred miles and which ones pay the best on which days. It could take me twenty minutes or twenty years, but I'll track her down.

I have Anise climb the stairs first so I can throw the caps up to her.

"Nash!" She yells down excitedly. "The cargo craft is still here!"

She hasn't left yet! Is my first thought until I consider why now. *This can't be good.*

I set some caps down, cover them in mushy garbage bags, and grab the bags of bots sitting next to the craft. I climb up and put the bags next to the matching trash bags, noting their location.

I see the craft parked right where we left it. My wrist controls are still linked to it, but so are Shae's. *How could I have trusted her so much?* It doesn't matter right now.

"I think my trip to Mecha just got fast-tracked, and the passenger ticket just got exchanged." I wink to Anise, who's smiling through a dirt covered face.

Wherever Shae is, she won't be gone for long, and based on the last thing she said to me, I'm afraid she'll have company. She knows too much about us, so we can't go home. Our only hope is to hop in a caravan as soon as possible and pay for protection.

I look at Anise, waiting for some kind of rebuttal, but she just nods. "Lead the way, big brother."

I open the cargo hatch to find there is some space still available. Since we're likely not coming back, I put the rest of the caps and the bag of bots in, regretting the hasty decision to cover them in stinking trash.

We do our best to push the dumpster back and conceal our path, though it's probably a waste of time.

Anise secures everything as I get in the driver seat. Transportation is usually automated, but I choose to override it manually. As I ease out onto the street, I realize that my plan has a big issue, the same one that made me think I could catch Shae. We can't make a quick getaway. Not only are these crafts slow, but I have to be extra careful with such sensitive cargo, my sister included.

As I scan the street, something hardens in my stomach like the concrete in the mixer we just blew up.

Despite being a quarter mile away, I recognize that form. Shae is back, and as I feared, she's not alone.

CHAPTER NINE

"Find some small caps, whatever you have," I instruct.

Anise is basically a brand new girl from the frail creature I almost had to carry from home this evening. She jumps to action and searches every cubby and then the cargo area.

"I can't find anything. All we have are the supercharged ones."

While I count how many slim-caps I have left, a swat lands on the view panel, then another.

They're attracted to the power.

Even though we have a small head start, there's no way we're outrunning Shae in her enhanced suit, unless I push this cargo craft to its limit. By doing that, I'm not just risking our safety, but possibly this entire city block.

The alternative is getting caught by Shae and the siphoners, and that could be worse than death.

I push the accelerator, easing up to a higher speed. I start blaring the warning horns and lights to clear any perps in our way. I hear the tinkling of caps as they tickle one another, innocent flirtations before a volatile relationship, and it reminds me of the times Shae and I bumped into each other while jogging and talking. Now I realize those little jolts of electricity I felt were probably just her advanced tech sucking my power away.

I still can't believe this young woman—who is catching up at an incredible pace—is a siphoner in disguise. She may or may not be logged in the system, but she has a crew of siphoners around her who aren't taking power from her, so that must mean she's in charge.

"Get the bag of bots." I say. "And close the cargo area. If one of those swatts gets too close to a cap, well, you know what could happen."

She looks at the window, which now has half a dozen swatts on it. If we get out of this, I'll have to figure out how to keep these things away. They're like a big flashing sign that says, "POWER OVER HERE!"

I glance at the video feed on the bottom of the view panel and see Shae within a hundred yards.

I push the top hatch above just enough for a bot to fly in. I slam it shut and yell, "Grab it, quick!"

We both reach frantically for the bug.

"Don't let it near the bag of bots!"

The cargo craft rocks, and I try to straighten the wheel, making it lurch the other way. I'd rather fight our pursuants than the craft. I focus on keeping the bag of bots safe while Anise grabs at the air just behind the swatt.

I consider setting the craft to automated travel, but it won't allow me to override the speed limiters. Automated travel is strictly governed and painfully slow. It's not worth getting caught, so I stay in the driver seat. We're only two miles away, which is about four minutes at this rate.

We can fight them off for four minutes, right?

Anise catches the swatt. "Got it! Now what?"

"We're gonna try something stupid," I say as I glance down at the bag of over-saturated bots.

"Are you kidding me?"

I shake my head. "Grab one of the supercharged bots, but keep them separated. We'll have to make this quick. If more swatts get in, this could be a disaster."

When she gets one out, I open the cargo area, push the bag into it, and seal the port.

"Whenever you're ready," I say as I watch Shae approaching. I know her caps will run out of power eventually, but she'll be able to jump on board in a matter of seconds.

"And by 'whenever'--" I slap the control to open the top hatch, "I mean 'now'!"

Anise pops her head out of the roof, smashes the bots together, and tosses them back.

I stare at the screen to see Shae leap toward the cargo craft. Then, we hear a familiar boom, and our cabin is filled with light from the flash.

"That worked?!" I say as Anise lowers herself back in and closes the hatch. A handful of bug bots made it in and are clamoring to get to the cargo area. They're powerless to do so, but we'll have to dispose of them soon.

Anise rubs her eyes. "Yeah, as soon as the dry-swatt linked with the super-swatt and tried to pull its power, they both exploded. I didn't see what happened to Shae though. I don't think she got on the craft, but she'll be back.

Part of me wonders if she's okay. I don't really want her to be hurt . . . too badly.

"And there are more coming."

I glance at the monitor to verify. I see Shae on the ground, and I nearly hit the brakes.

She made her choice, I remind myself. Then, something like joy is replaced with something like fear as I see her push herself up slowly. She doesn't seem too energetic, but her friends do.

Half a dozen siphoners—even a few people dressed like Shae—are approaching quickly.

One mile to go.

"You know what to do," I say with a smile.

Anise bags up the dry bots before opening the cargo area. She retrieves one supercharged swatt at a time, making sure to seal the bot-bag into the cargo area each time more swatts come in.

The explosions vary in force and timing.

"Be careful!" I yell, knowing Anise is doing everything she can to help.

I wish she wasn't the one risking blowing her hands off, but she doesn't know how to drive. I barely know how, and I'm surprised I haven't blown us up with all the jostling.

Only two more siphoners are still chasing us. The road is littered with a handful of injured siphoners who got too close to a swatt bomb.

I can barely see ahead because of all the bug-bots, and the cabin is filling up with them again. I have no choice but to switch to auto-drive and help Anise.

When I do, the location counter doubles, and we're now two minutes away again.

"How many super-swatts are left?" I ask as I gather the dry-swatts.

"I don't know, maybe three or four."

That should work, I think.

At only fifteen miles per hour, the last two siphoners could catch up any second. I quickly snatch two super-swatts this time in one hand while holding two dry-swatts in the other.

"Get ready," I say to Anise as we make eye contact. Something about working together with someone your whole life allows these moments where words aren't as necessary.

I nod, and she slams her hand against the hatch button. I push my hands out first, smashing all four bots together, then stand up to find my target. It looks like only one siphoner had the energy and resilience to keep chasing, and he's still twenty feet away.

I realize what a waste it was, but there's no time for remorse now. I throw the swatt-bomb and drop back into the craft.

This time, the explosion is big enough to push the craft forward, and I hear the other caps tapping one another in the back again. I know we packed it full, but now that they've settled, there's a little space between many of them.

I land back in the driver seat, glancing at the rear monitor. The camera has been destroyed, so it's just a blank feed, but I know we're in the clear.

Just to be safe, I take back controls and double our speed.

An overlaying message pops up on the map screen, "Now entering Caravan Safe Zone."

"Alright, Sis, looks like our trip to the holy land got fast-tracked. Let's hope things slow down soon."

"For some reason," Anise responds, "I don't think they will."

END

Join the next adventure at michaellacey.me.

You found this book. You read a review or heard something about it that encouraged you to download and read it.

That is the power of words.

Now, I need you to use *your power, your words*. Help more people find these stories.

Leave a review on the platforms you use.

Who knows, maybe enough excitement will spur a series, or a movie?! (*Seriously, this is a dream goal of mine, so if anyone has connections, let me know!*)

Thank you for joining me in these wonderful fictitious worlds that sometimes feel a bit too real. I truly hope you are changed for the better after reading my words.

-M. Lacey

Michael writes under a few other names: M. Lacey for fiction, Michael Lacey for nonfiction (mostly devotional and inspirational religious writings), and Ray Scar as a pen name for his Quick Six series (due to some unsavory characters and situations).

As an emerging author of genre bending books, he's always looking to bring something new to the scene. If you want another book like "insert popular title here," you probably won't find that in Michael's backlist, but you're sure to find something unique, entertaining, hopefully inventive, and inspiring.

Story is powerful. It changes lives, sometimes for a moment, sometimes for eternity.

Michael's goal is to take readers to the edge of the human experience and then cross the line. If that sounds like something you want, it's time to read. Sign up for more short stories, advance releases, and updates from Michael at fiction.MichaelLacey.me.

Find more at MichaelLacey.me.

ALSO BY M. LACEY_

VISIT MICHAELLACEY.ME/LIBRARY FOR LINKS TO THESE BOOKS AND STORIES!

1. *The Luminant Series (formerly A Town Called Wonderful)*

Full length novels following Luka's journey as he learns of his heritage and abilities as a Luminant, a traveller of underlands throughout the earth. His childhood friend, Quinn, becomes so much more in their harrowing quests together as they search for Luka's parents and truths around the mysterious underlands.

Underlands are organisms themselves but also house ancient civilizations are the root of most current mythology, from creatures like behemoths, leviathans, and chupacabras to fabled lands of El Dorado, Atlantis, and the Fountain of Youth.

2. *Short Stories and More Series*

Like *Perpetual*? You'll also enjoy other shorts ranging from a flash fiction at few words to Novelette lengths at 16k+ words.

Michael sends new stories exclusively to his subscriber list. Join and follow along.

Invite other readers: fiction.MichaelLacey.me

COLLABORATIONS

Michael loves to collaborate. These stories will be sent to his mailing list, but they can be found in the compilations below as well.

Connect with Michael at michael@michaellacey.me if you have an anthology idea or want to participate in one yourself. If he can't make it work, he has the connections you need for every part of the book production process.

3. "Thirteen's Last Christmas" exists in the same universe as Lacey's Luminant series. It is a standalone short story, a creative 'saving Christmas' adventure. It can also be found in the collection, *Untold Christmas Stories: 12 Different Tales from 12 Different Genres*.

4. A global pandemic changes everything. What happens next? "Remnant, A Post-Pandemic Dystopian Tale" is the survival journal of two siblings after the fourth wave of this disease has swept the United States, and possibly the world. You can find this story in the collection *Six Feet From Tomorrow: Post Pandemic Tales of What Could Be*.

DEVOTIONAL WORKS BY MICHAEL LACEY

While Michael's fiction work isn't Christian fiction, he is a Christian who writes fiction. He shares encouraging devotionals and inspirational writings under his full name: Michael Lacey.

5. Hope When it Hurts: The Scars that Shape Us (A Christian Writers' Collection, more info at ChristWriters.com)

It's easy to lose hope, especially in today's world. Through times like these, we all need to be reminded of the *hope of Jesus!*

Hope for the Moment is a collection of what we're calling **Devotional Stories**, *real stories* by *real people* about a *real God.* There are some heavy moments, but in every story, hope is found and God is glorified. These serve to remind of God's *faithfulness* and *goodness.*

While most of the Christian writers in this collection are women, it can serve to encourage *anyone* of *any age.* Writers from around the world have contributed to this collaboration. We celebrate the international feel and have retained author styles.

May the real stories from these real people reflect the real God and **add HOPE to your season**. ***There is hope,*** a *living hope* in Jesus, one that *does not disappoint.*

*Half of the proceeds go to support Star of Hope.

5. As We Fight: A Weekly Guide Through the Warfare of Worship

Relevant and Timely Encouragements! (now comes with FREE Audiobook!)

As your church service approaches the same time every week, **are you struggling to make time** for spiritual preparation?

Does worship sometimes feel more like a **task than an expression?**

Do you often feel **alone in your pursuits as a leader or worshiper?**

This *well organized and timely book* delivers tried and tested wisdom that will strengthen your leadership and encourage your team. It will save you time with its succinct, season-specific devotionals in ONE easy-to-access place.

This book contains affiliate links. Babies gotta eat!

"REMNANT" SAMPLE_

SURVIVAL JOURNAL_

This is my survival journal, from COVID-19 being the first wave in 2020 to this cancerous fourth wave crushing what remains of us in late 2021. Based on the fact that I'm in the top 10% of survivors—not that there's much competition—I might be someone worth listening to.

If we'd only known that the coronavirus was just the beginning, maybe we would've survived the next three waves. Then again, it's impossible to know. Dad said it was pointless to think of what could have happened, because that's not a productive use of our precious time.

That's the funny part—not the kind to make us laugh, not much does that anymore—no, I mean the fact that time is all we seemed to have had during the initial wave of the coronavirus. And no, it was not followed by the Bud Light virus or the Dos Equis virus...I doubt the people that made those kinds of jokes made it past the second wave.

I remember hearing about someone who came home coughing up blood after a week of having the coronavirus —that's the same thing as COVID-19, it's hard to remember those little things with everything that followed. The crazy thing is that she had gone to the doctor a week before and been tested for flu and all kinds of stuff, except corona, and then sent home.

And that's how everything else went. We didn't know what we were looking for until it was too late. In fact, by looking for those things, we made it worse, and the spread was so much faster, wider.

-Remy

SEPTEMBER-ISH, 2021_

- charger and cable
- phone - triple check
- magazine, paper
- magazine, clip
- trade for whatever food we can get

Micah,

You keep interrupting me. I'm trying to write this FOR you. You're too young to understand it all, at least, that's what I tell myself. Maybe I'm just not ready to tell you.

You broke the rules, so we have to leave again. Not that his community was that great, but it was safe.

I'm sure you don't remember this, but I told you not to show our pre-fallout pictures to other kids. You know exactly why, and it's very important they don't see what you looked like before. We won't have to follow these rules much longer, but I can't tell you that. Poor kid, you can't keep a secret to save your...well, you know. And these days, that truly is the power of secrets.

I can't blame you completely.

"It's a waste of resources," someone said when they caught me using a laptop to edit some photos, but the lady didn't just say it like a fact. She said it like she wished I would leave, like I'm toxic to her little vision of paradise.

If you ask me, and no one does, I think we need pictures, reminders. We need art and joy. Honestly, we need to be able to waste something. I know, that doesn't sound good in times like this.

It's probably a good thing you're fast-forwarding our stay here. It's a matter of time before they're raided, though 'conquered' might be a better word. And we do not want to be around for another one of those, especially not you, little one.

That last escape cost more than it was worth. This time, Micah, you may have just saved our lives. I've got you packing our bags already, though you I know you don't want to leave.

"But, I just made friends, and there's this girl who's really nice, and she showed me her picture when she was pretty and I wanted to show her..."

"That's enough." I had to interrupt you. I don't like doing it, and I know exactly how it feels.

When Dad did it, I stared fire through him—not to be confused with the third wave, of course. And now, I find myself doing it to you. Now I know why, it's because I know something you don't, lots actually. But I still don't know enough.

Maybe if I'd filled my head with words rather than images, I'd have a better idea of how to handle these thi—

And...I just had to chase you down. You tried to run away, again. Or tried to run back into the town. For a smart nine-year-old, you're not very bright, which is more proof that my plan is a good one. Where did you think you were going to go? Then came the part you might actually remember, a switching. I don't like to do it, but you're almost as stubborn as me, and I know what it took to keep me in line.

Whatever it takes, I'm going to get you to Sam's—no, not the giant store, every one of which was raided during the second wave (some might say they were raided during COVID, but that was child's play to what came next).

Being without Dad is hard. Sorry, I zoned out for a minute and thought about him again. You may not be able to tell, but I'm barely holding it together. If someone asked me how, I would say, "I don't have a choice. It has to be done."

I sure miss him. I know you do too. I had more time with both of them than you, but a hundred years wouldn't be enough.

-Remy

[get the rest of the book on Amazon now]